Go For It, Carrie

Lesley Choyce

Go For It, Carrie

Illustrations by Mark Thurman

FIRST NOVELS

The New Series

Formac Publishing Limited
Halifax, Nova Scotia

Formac Publishing Company Limited acknowledges the sup-
port of the Canada Council and the Nova Scotia Department
of Education and Culture in the development of writing and
publishing in Canada.

Canadian Cataloguing in Publication Data

Choyce, Lesley

Go for it, Carrie

(First novel series)

ISBN 0-88780-392-X (pbk.) ISBN 0-88780-393-8 (bound)

I. Thurman, Mark, 1948– II. Title. III. Series.

PS8555.H668G59 1997   jC813'.54   C96-950185-4
PZ7.C448Go 1997

Formac Publishing Limited
5502 Atlantic Street
Halifax, NS B3H 1G4

Printed and bound in Canada.

Table of Contents

For Pamela

1
Like Ice

My brother Ernie was supposed to stay home with me after school. But it didn't usually work out that way.

"I hate being a baby sitter," he said.

"I don't need a baby sitter!" I snapped. "I'm no baby. I'm ten years old."

"Right. Let's get out of here and see what Joe is doing."

What Joe was doing was standing around on the sidewalk. "Hey, Ernie," Joe said. "What's happening with you, man? Why'd you bring the little kid?"

Ernie looked like he wanted me to get lost. "Don't be bothering us, okay?" he told me.

I just smiled and then stuck out my tongue at both of them. I decided that when I got home I would hide Ernie's Walkman just to cause him some grief.

Right then, from out of nowhere, some guy on rollerblades came whizzing by on the sidewalk at about a hundred kilometres an hour. He jumped the curb, skated up the wheelchair ramp on the side of the library and disappeared down a side street.

"Cool," Joe said.

"Like ice," Ernie added.

Suddenly the words jumped out of my mouth.

"I could do that."

I had this picture in my head of me cruising down the sidewalk like the wind.

Joe laughed real loud and Ernie snorted, "No way, little sister."

"You're too young," Joe said. "Besides, where would you get the money to buy those things?"

But I knew I *could* rollerblade like the wind if I only had the chance to try.

"Just wait," I said.

2
Nothing Makes a Difference

"Nothing I do seems to make any difference," my mom said as she came in through the door. "I'd quit that job if we didn't need the money to live on."

I wanted to ask if I could have a pair of roller-blades. But the timing was bad. Instead, I gave her a hug.

"Did Ernie do a good job?" my mom asked.

"I'm doing an excellent job, Mom," Ernie answered.

"That true, Carrie?"

"We're doing okay," I said.

My mom set a newspaper down on the table and walked out of the room. I picked it up and flipped to the hockey scores.

That's when I saw the ad. *"On sale this week. Only $79.95."*

"Wow," was all I could say.

My brother was behind me now. "Seventy-nine ninety-five," he read out and then snickered.

"What's seventy-nine ninety-five?" my mother asked.

"Nothing, Mom," I said. I tucked the paper under my arm and walked to my bedroom. I could see myself cruising down the sidewalk, feeling the wind on my face. But how could I possibly ask my mother for the

HERO.
ON SALE THIS WEEK
$79.95

money to buy a pair of roller-blades?

I pulled an envelope out of my socks drawer and opened it. I knew how much was in it but I had to check just in case some miracle had happened.

But not this time. Two five dollar bills.

"Two times five is ten," I said out loud.

Then I looked at the ad in the newspaper. This time I didn't see anything but the price: $79.95.

I ripped out the page and crumpled it up into a ball.

"It's not fair," I said to no one.

3
Bad Day at School

I was having a bad day in school. When my teacher asked me a math question I didn't know the answer. I tried to pay attention but nothing worked. A guy named Gregory sat alongside of me. Gregory had Down's syndrome and was new in school this year. Some kids made fun of him, but I thought he was cool. He had a way of making you smile no matter what was going wrong.

Gregory wrote something on a piece of paper and passed it to me.

"*Hi.*"

That's all it said, nothing more. Gregory smiled and gave me two thumbs up. I suddenly felt a whole lot better.

Well, I felt a whole lot better until the teacher came walking down the aisle.

"I can tell that *some* of you aren't interested in math today." She looked at Gregory, looked at me, and then picked up the note on my desk.

"I think it's time for a pop quiz," she said.

As she turned to go to the board, Gregory gave me a thumbs down.

Out in the playground, I knew I had failed the quiz. My mind just wasn't on school. I pulled out the crumpled newspaper ad

that I had been carrying in my pocket. Gregory sat down beside me and smoothed it out with his hands. He looked at it real close.

"Go for it," was all he said.

4
A Dangerous Place for a Kid with Money

Walking home from school, I passed by old Mr. Lawrence's pawnshop. All kinds of junk was piled in the window. I was almost past the store when I realized what I had seen.

I walked backwards, slowly, afraid that they might disappear. In the window was a pair of the most beat-up looking kids' roller-blades that I had ever seen in my life. Maybe I was dreaming.

I opened the door to the shop. A little bell rang overhead, and old Mr. Lawrence looked up.

"In the window," was all I could say.

"Yes, what about the window?" Mr. Lawrence sounded annoyed.

"The roller-blades," I stammered. "How much?"

"Oh, those old things. Twenty bucks and they're yours."

Twenty dollars was still way too much. I said nothing else. The bell rang on the door again when I left.

At home, Ernie had left a mess on the kitchen table from his afternoon snack. He had given up trying to find his Walkman and had gone to play basketball. I went to my room and counted my money. Two times five was still ten. Holding the money in my hands, though, a picture of Gregory's smiling face floated into my head.

"Go for it," I heard myself whispering. I folded the money in half and put it in my shoe.

I was just barely out the front door when I ran into Joe. "Carrie, you wouldn't happen to have some change on you so I could play a video game?"

I shook my head no.

Joe looked hard into my face. "I hope you're not lying to me."

Joe was scaring me now. I didn't have Ernie here to protect me. But I wouldn't give him a cent.

"Sorry, Joe. I can't help you."

I ran for it down the street. When I arrived at the pawn shop, the little bell rang and it sounded like a fire alarm in my head.

"Not you again," old Mr. Lawrence said. "I don't like kids hanging out in my store."

"Would you take ten dollars for the roller-blades?" I blurted out.

"You don't have ten dollars," Mr. Lawrence snapped.

I took off my shoe and showed it to him.

Mr. Lawrence looked at me like I was totally weird.

"They're worth twenty," he said. "Didn't you see the price?"

I felt scared but I mustered my courage.

"Would you take ten? It's all I have."

"You must think I'm crazy," he answered.

Just then, I was sure that Mr. Lawrence was crazy. He was that scary.

"Please," I whispered.

Mr. Lawrence looked up at the ceiling. Then he threw up his hands. "Put the money on the counter."

He walked past me, yanked the roller-blades from the pile of junk in the window and set them on the floor in front of me. I was ready to jump out of my skin with excitement.

Mr. Lawrence picked up some elbow and knee pads lying in the corner and threw them at my feet. "You might as well take these as well," he said gruffly. "Keep you from getting all scraped up."

5
The Harder You Try, the Harder You Fall

I headed for the empty parking lot beside the supermarket. It would be a good place to try out my wheels. I also knew this was where Gregory might be hanging out, but when I got there I was too nervous to even talk to him. I sat down, put the roller-blades on and tightened the laces. I was so excited that my hands were shaking.

The first time I tried to stand up, my feet flew out from under me. *Wham!* It was a hard landing on the asphalt. Gregory rushed over to help me up. I got on my feet again and wobbled. When I tried to roll forward, I rolled backward. When I tried to roll backward, I rolled forward.

I finally rolled a little ways with my arms swinging all over the place. Then my wheels hit some stones and sent me flying. That's when I realized I had an audience of more than one.

Ernie and Joe were there. "I've been looking for you," Ernie said. He seemed mad about something.

"Here I am," I said. I stood up but my legs flew out from under me again. *Wham!* Back on the pavement. Then Ernie and Joe laughed.

"You'll never be able to do it," Ernie said.

Joe laughed. Then all of a sudden he looked serious. "Where did *you* get the money to buy those things?"

"None of your business," I sassed back.

Ernie was just shaking his head as they walked off. "That kid can't do anything right," I heard him saying to Joe.

Gregory came over to help me onto my feet.

"Thanks," I said. I tried getting the hang of rolling again, but just couldn't do it.

I had been fooling myself. My brother was right. "I guess I just wasted my life savings," I told Gregory as I started to unlace the roller-blades.

Gregory shook his head. "No way," he said. "You can do it. Go for it."

But I was already hurting from all the times I had fallen. I was ready to throw the rollerblades in the trash. But Gregory was right there, so I didn't.

"See ya later," I said.

6
I Can Do Anything

When my mom came home I didn't want to tell her about buying a pair of roller-blades I couldn't use.

All night long I heard the voice of my brother in my head: "You'll never be able to do it. You'll never be able to do it." Why did Ernie have to be so mean?

When the sun woke me up in the morning, though, I realized that Ernie's voice wasn't banging around in my head any more. I *wasn't* ready to give up.

I got up out of bed like lightning and ran downstairs.

It was Saturday. No school. I gulped down breakfast and wrote a note for my mom. The parking lot was only half a block away. I had to go there — that was all there was to it.

First, I put on the left foot. Then I put on the right. I was concentrating hard when I stood up, hanging onto the wall. Now I was up. I moved one foot, wobbled, then moved the other. *Push. Glide. Push. Glide. Push. Glide. Glide.* I was going around in a circle but I was rolling. Wow!

I've got it. Now I can roller-blade without even falling. I can do anything! I thought. I had to steady myself.

There was a gently sloping concrete ramp alongside the empty supermarket. I held onto the railing as I made my way to the top. Then I turned around and raced straight down without hardly thinking. It felt great.

I went back to the top and did it again, this time cruising right out into the middle of the parking lot. I did it again and again, and it all felt so wonderful.

All I could think about was proving to Ernie that he was wrong. That's when I raced down the ramp at top speed, tucked in low and screamed out into the middle of the parking lot towards the street.

Suddenly, a car turned off the street into the empty parking lot. It was all happening so fast.

I couldn't stop. I was headed straight towards it.

"Help!" I screamed. The guy driving slammed on his brakes. *Screech!* Just as I was about to hit the bumper, I dove off to the side and landed hard on some broken bricks.

"Ouch!" I had a hard time getting my breath.

The man jumped out of his car. "Are you all right?" he yelled. He looked really scared.

"I think so," I said.

"You could have been killed," he screamed at me.

"I'm sorry," I said. I suddenly realized how close I'd come to getting hurt, maybe even killed.

The man backed out of the parking lot and left. I sat there

for a few minutes feeling really shaken.

Joe was walking by just then and saw me sitting on the broken bricks where I had wiped out. He laughed out loud.

"Give it up, Carrie. You'll never get it."

But I knew that I wouldn't quit.

7
All Gregory's Fault

When I showed up at Gregory's door wearing my roller-blades, Gregory's mother looked quite surprised.

"Can Gregory come with me for a little while?"

Gregory's mom looked at the roller-blades again and then at me. I smiled a big smile. "I think that would be okay," she said.

Gregory was so excited when he saw me roll down the side-walk that he jumped up and down and clapped his hands like I had just performed a miracle.

When we arrived back at the parking lot, Gregory ran alongside as I cruised up and down the ramp and made loops in the parking lot. "Go for it!" he shouted.

I never fell once this time. With Gregory watching, I had all the confidence in the world. When I finally got tired, I sat down on the pavement and Gregory sat down beside me. "Wow!" he said. "You're good."

My feet were hurting so I took off the roller-blades. Gregory picked one up and began to spin the wheels. And then he said something surprising.

"Can I try?" he asked.

I wasn't expecting that. I didn't know what to say. Gregory was my friend, a good friend. But he

was also someone with Down's syndrome. Sometimes he could be pretty clumsy. What could I say to keep from hurting his feelings?

"They probably wouldn't fit you," I said.

But Gregory was already sticking his foot into the roller-blade. And then he smiled. It fit. He put his other foot in and began to lace them both up.

When Gregory was ready to stand up, I said, "Well, okay. Just hang onto me." I helped Gregory to stand and caught him as he began to wobble. He rolled one way and then another and I couldn't hold onto him.

I sat him back down and put my knee pads and elbow pads on

him just in case. Then Gregory suddenly got up on his feet and tried to skate off across the parking lot. He didn't get far before he went crashing down.

Gregory tried again and fell again. He didn't want to give up. Over and over he stood up, took a step, and crashed onto the pavement. *This is never going to work*, I was thinking. I should never have let him even try. I was really afraid he was going to get hurt.

When I saw Joe coming back with my brother Ernie, I knew I had to put a stop to this. "Forget it, Gregory," I said. "I'm sorry. Take them off."

Gregory sat down and looked very hurt. I knew how Gregory was feeling but he was making me feel rotten too. This wasn't fair. I had been having a great time. Now I felt rotten. And it was all Gregory's fault.

8
You Have to Know
Your Limits

I didn't invite Gregory back to watch me the next day. First, I cleared off some of the stones and broken glass. Next, I went racing around the lot in a figure eight. Now I liked it when people stopped on the sidewalk to watch my moves.

I really wished Ernie and Joe could see me now. I decided I would just have to go to them and show them what I could do.

The sidewalks were crowded and people were in my way.

"Coming through!" I yelled.

"Hey, better slow down," one woman with groceries said to me.

"Watch where you're going," an old man screeched when I bumped into him.

But instead of slowing down, I went faster. I dodged a pop can and a big crack in the sidewalk and a little kid in a stroller.

When I arrived at the corner, Ernie and Joe were just standing there gawking at me.

Ernie scrunched up his nose and said, "How did you learn to do that?"

"Practice," I said, rolling around in perfect circles.

Joe had his hockey stick and tried to trip me. "Bet you're not as good as you think you are," he said.

"Wrong," I said and raced up and down the sidewalk as fast as I could.

"Hey, take it easy," Ernie said. He looked a little worried.

Joe tapped his hockey stick on the concrete. "That's just little kid stuff. That's nothing." I knew that Joe was holding a grudge because I hadn't given him any money to play his video game. "See that wall over there?" He pointed to a metre high brick wall that went around the park. It was flat on top and maybe half a metre wide.

"So?"

"So if you're so good, I want to see you make it from one end to the other as fast as you can go."

I looked at the wall. Could I roller-blade on something that narrow? I was feeling like I could do anything.

"Don't be stupid, Carrie," Ernie said and grabbed me by the elbow.

"I can do it," I insisted.

"I'm not going to *let* you do it!" he shouted.

"Why do you care?"

"I care because I don't want to see you get hurt."

All of a sudden he was leading me down the street along that brick wall. I didn't get it. My brother had never cared what happened to me before. When we were half a block away, Ernie picked me up and sat me on top of the wall. "Now try standing up," he said.

I got up onto my feet okay but the top of the wall was way too narrow. First one foot slipped off and then another. As I started to fall, my brother grabbed me before I went *splat* on the concrete.

"You have to know your limits," Ernie said. "If someone dares you to do something stupid, don't do it."

9
Born on Roller-blades

At school, Gregory was his old self again — smiling, happy, giving me a thumbs up during a spelling test. After school I headed for the empty parking lot with my roller-blades. Gregory tagged along. I was thinking, *Oh no. He's going to ask to try again.*

He sat down and watched as I laced them up. I felt guilty for not offering him another chance. I took them off. "Here," I said. "Try again. You can't always get it the first time."

Gregory shook his head. "I can't do it," he said. "You're good. Not me. Go for it."

I knew I was good. And Gregory was smiling. He was okay. He'd be happy to just watch. Yet suddenly I didn't feel like showing off. I handed the roller-blades to Gregory.

"The trick," I said, "is to learn one little thing at a time."

Gregory smiled but then looked a little scared.

"You can do it, Gregory. I know you can."

And with that, Gregory put on the roller-blades and the pads. I helped him stand up. "Now just take one small step and glide."

Gregory took a small step, rolled, let go of me, and went about one metre before crashing down. I helped him up and he tried again. And again. And again. Each time he went a little further before he fell.

Fortunately, he was learning to fall so that it didn't hurt. To anyone else watching, he looked like a disaster on wheels. I knew, though, that he was getting the hang of it. That's when I noticed that some adults had stopped on the sidewalk and were watching.

"He can't learn to do that," somebody yelled.

Gregory fell again and when he looked up, he saw the adults looking at him. This time he didn't get up.

When I ran over to help him up, Gregory acted like he didn't *want* to get up again.

"Forget about them," I said. "Now get up and go for it."

I helped Gregory back onto his feet. He took a small step and glided. He took a big step and glided. Pretty soon he was cruising all the way across the parking lot past the people on the sidewalk. He never even looked at them. He just kept moving his feet and looking straight ahead like he'd been born on roller-blades and skating all his life.

10
Nothing to It

The next time Gregory's mother opened the door and saw me with my roller-blades hanging over my shoulder, she had a big scowl on her face.

"Are you the one who put the idea into his head?"

"What idea?" I asked.

"He asked his father and me if we could buy him a pair of those things." She pointed to my roller-blades.

I wasn't surprised that Gregory wanted his own roller-blades. I'd been sharing mine with him nearly every day now for a week.

"He learned pretty quick. You should see him."

"You mean he can actually do it? I thought he was making it up."

I shook my head no.

"I still think it's too dangerous. What if he gets hurt?"

"I'll teach him to know his limits."

Gregory was at the door now beside his mother.

"I don't think it's a good thing for Gregory," his mother said.

I figured I had to do something. I handed the roller-blades to Gregory. His mom looked worried but didn't say no.

"I think you should show her what you can do," I said to Gregory.

Gregory put on the pads and the blades and stood nervously outside the back door. His mother held her breath as he clumsily rolled over the rough walkway, but when he got to the paved driveway, he turned around and smiled.

Suddenly, Gregory took a big step and glided down the steep driveway. He pushed off harder, racing away from the house towards the street where traffic was rushing by.

"Gregory!" his frantic mother screamed.

But Gregory had no intention of doing anything dangerous. He made a neat U-turn and then

kicked up his foot to put on the brake. He came to a full stop and was looking back at his mom. He held his hands up in the air as if to say, *Nothing to it.* Then he rolled back up the driveway and up to the door.

Gregory's mom gave him a hug.

"Thanks, Carrie," Gregory said.

I smiled at Gregory and his mom. "We both knew we could do it if we just kept trying," I said. "All we had to do was go for it."

Meet five other great kids in the New First Novels Series:

• Meet Morgan the Magician
in *Morgan Makes Magic*
by Ted Staunton/Illustrated by Bill Slavin
When he's in a tight spot, Morgan tells stories — and most of them stretch the truth, to say the least. But when he tells kids at his new school he can do magic tricks, he really gets in trouble — most of all with the dreaded Aldeen Hummel!

• Meet Jan the Curious
in *Jan's Big Bang*
by Monica Hughes/Illustrated by Carlos Friere
Taking part in the Science Fair is a big deal for Grade Three kids, but Jan and her best friend Sarah are ready for the challenge. Still, finding a safe project isn't easy, and the girls discover that getting ready for the fair can cause a whole lot of trouble.

• Meet Robyn the Dreamer
in *Shoot for the Moon, Robyn*
by Hazel Hutchins/ Illustrated by Yvonne Cathcart
When the teacher asks her to sing for the class, Robyn knows it's her chance to be

the world's best singer. Should she perform like Celine Dion, or do *My Bonnie Lies Over the Ocean*, or the matchmaker song? It's hard to decide, even for the world's best singer — and the three boys who throw spitballs don't make it any easier.

- **Meet Duff the Daring**
  in *Duff the Giant Killer*
  by Budge Wilson/Illustrated by Kim LaFave
  Getting over the chicken pox can be boring, but Duff and Simon find a great way to enjoy themselves — acting out one of their favourite stories, *Jack the Giant Killer*, in the park. In fact, they do it so well the police get into the act.

- **Meet Lilly the Bossy**
  in *Lilly to the Rescue*
  by Brenda Bellingham/ Illustrated by Kathy Kaulbach
  Bossy-boots! That's what kids at school start calling Lilly when she gives a lot of advice that's not wanted. Lilly can't help telling people what to do — but how can she keep any of her friends if she always knows better?

Look for these First Novels!

- *About Arthur*
  Arthur Throws a Tantrum
  Arthur's Dad
  Arthur's Problem Puppy

- *About Fred*
  Fred and the Stinky Cheese
  Fred's Dream Cat

- *About the Loonies*
  Loonie Summer
  The Loonies Arrive

- *About Maddie*
  Maddie in Hospital
  Maddie Goes to Paris
  Maddie in Danger
  Maddie in Goal
  Maddie Wants Music
  That's Enough Maddie!

- *About Mikey*
  Good For You, Mikey Mite!
  Mikey Mite Goes to School
  Mikey Mite's Big Problem

- *About Mooch*
  Mooch Forever
  Hang On, Mooch!
  Mooch Gets Jealous
  Mooch and Me

- *About the Swank Twins*
  The Swank Prank
  Swank Talk

- *About Max*
  Max the Superhero

Formac Publishing Company Limited
5502 Atlantic Street, Halifax, Nova Scotia B3H 1G4
Orders: 1-800-565-1975 Fax: (902) 425-0166